Music of Seduction

Ashley Brion

Published by Ashley Brion, 2024.

MUSIC OF SEDUCTION

First edition. May 21, 2024.

Written by Ashley Brion.

Also by Ashley Brion

Brooke de Láuront
The Black Rogue
Letters From Home
Secrets in Paris

Standalone
Caged With A Rebel
Birth of the Wicked
Illusion at Midnight
The Mashed Potato Incident
What Once Was
Music of Seduction

Watch for more at https://www.slucas0.wixsite.com/
authorashleybrion.

Author's Note

Ever since I was a small child I have been OBSESSED with the mafia. I grew up on movies like *The Godfather, Goodfellas, Casino, Donnie Brasco, Prizzi's Honor*, and *Scarface*. I absolutely loved the history of the real-life gangsters, especially Al Capone. I thought maybe one day I'd grow up and become a hitman for the mob. Great dreams for a kid, right? Well, I may have grew out of the actual wanting to be in the mob phase (sort of) but my fascination with it hasn't wavered. Hell, I even started studying the Chinese Triad and Japanese Yakuza.

Now, do I know members of the Italian mafia? Sure do. Will I say more than that? Fuck no. I have *some* semblance of smarts rolling around in this bone-covered meat sack of mine. Granted, not sure if the idea for this was clever or not.

The story started out as a typical anthology sign-up for my friend and fellow author Quell T. Fox who runs Fluffy Fox Publishing. A dark romance centered around a villain falling in love? Sign me the *fuck* up. That's when I had the idea to make it a dark mafia romance, but I had no idea on how to do a villain retelling. I immediately knew I wanted the MMC to be the villain, but what kind of vibes was I gonna give this guy? That's when it hit me: use one of my favorite villains of all time. Now of course some of you are probably thinking, *oh dear here she goes using The Joker*. HAHA! Not so fast mes amis. I happen to have a second favorite villain who I adore just as much, and it's not Harley Quinn either. I modeled Darius off of a very unknown B-list, hell you could even call him C-list, baddie in Batman's Rogue's Gallery: the Music Meister. Yep, Darius is modeled after that beautiful musical episode in *Batman: The Brave and the Bold* featuring Neil Patrick Harris' exquisite voice. I'm just happy we've gone from one-off villain in a 2009 musical episode to now being featured in other animated series plus got his own comic run! But enough of my rambling before I start to drool.

This is my first very major pepper rated story, so here goes! I thank all my lovely friends who I met on TikTok and my Smutty ass team who inspired me to write this story.

To my wonderful in-person friends, is this spicy enough for you fuckers now?

And to all the musical-loving friends who have fantasized themselves with so many masked and unmasked characters:

If only you could love me like I love villainy, baby girl. Now get your ass up on that piano and spread 'em.

Music of Seduction Playlist

BATMAN THE BRAVE AND the Bold: Mayhem of the Music Meister Soundtrack: Neil Patrick Harris, Grey DeLisle, James Arnold Taylor, John Di Maggio, et al.

Ain't That A Kick in the Head: Dean Martin

That's Amore: Dean Martin

Chain Gang: Sam Cooke

Buona sera (Signorina): Fred Buscaglione

The Godfather Parts I, II, and III Soundtracks: The City of Prague Philharmonic Orchestra

Chicago: Frank Sinatra

Moonlight Sonata: Ludwig van Beethoven

Symphony No. 5 in C Minor Op. 67: Ludwig van Beethoven

Symphony No. 5 in E Minor Op. 64: Ludwig van Beethoven

Symphony No. 9 in D Minor, Op. 125: Ludwig van Beethoven

Allegretto for String Quartet in B: Ludwig van Beethoven

Italian Restaurant for One: Italian Social Club

The Phantom of the Opera (Original 1987 Cast Recording): Andrew Lloyd Webber

Clair de Lune: Claude Debussy

Nocturne No. 2 in E-Flat Major, Op. 9 No. 2: Frédéric Chopin

Want to check out the Spotify playlist? You can copy the link here:

https://open.spotify.com/playlist/
4NklCuLY1wHTLsc6fXn2nL?si=cf806e4207294e57

Or scan the QR Code:

Darius

"FUCK." DARIUS GROWLED. He tapped his fingers on the side of his whiskey glass. He wasn't surprised this seedy, little, shit bar didn't have anything remotely passing as a delicacy. This cheap Jonnie Walker Blue would have to do. He gently swirled the amber liquid, the heady, sharp scent filling his nostrils. Taking a sip, he scrunched his nose and reluctantly swallowed.

Disgusting putrid shit.

Sitting in a booth near the bar, he remained in the shadows, out of sight from prying eyes. The smoky haze of cigars and cigarettes *hung in the air, setting like concrete in his lungs.* He checked his Philippe watch hidden under his white button-down sleeve.

Where the fuck is he...

Darius was positioned so he could see the front door and get a full view of the bar. His sharp eyes hidden under tinted glasses were pointed at the door when he saw his assistant walk in.

"Where the fuck have you been, Eddie?" he growled. "You were supposed to be here before me."

Eddie adjusted his leather jacket and smoothed over his thick black hair as he sat down. "Yeah, well, shit happens, *sir*."

That last word bit on the end of his tongue was laced with sarcasm and malice.

"Don't take that fucking tone with me, Eddie. Where've you been?"

Eddie signaled to the sexy blonde bartender to bring him a drink. "Lager, sweetheart."

Eddie looked back at Darius. "We've been here a fucking week looking for this guy and I finally found the son of a bitch. He's here alright. His girlfriend lives here, so he thought he could hide from us with her in fucking Bigfoot country. Stupid fuck."

Darius felt the corner of his mouth rise into a small smirk. "Taking off to bumfuck nowhere in the middle of the mountains. And the term is Appalachia, Eddie. Get educated for once."

The bartender breezed by their booth and sat the dark beer in front of Eddie. He took a big gulp and shook his head. "That's your job. I don't need education to find a fucking person."

Darius rolled his eyes. Eddie certainly had a way with words. He took a sip from his glass. "So where is he?"

"Don't know. But I know someone who does know."

"And who is that?"

Eddie arched his head toward the bar. "His girl is coming in here soon to meet up with some friends. We talk to her, we can talk to him."

Talk...sure. The word that no one else in the building would think twice was code for more nefarious deeds.

"You know my rules." Darius muttered.

"Sure do, boss. Wouldn't wanna talk her ear off. You know how personable I can be."

Darius furrowed his ginger brows. More code for beating the shit out of someone and torturing them until they talk. Women and children were off limits, and Eddie knew that. Even men in his line of work had morals. Most of them anyway.

Darius reached into his jeans pocket and pulled out his phone. He pressed a few buttons and Eddie's phone let out an obnoxious ding.

"You did good work. I'll take it from here."

Eddie downed his beer and placed the empty glass with dregs of froth on the table. "See you back in Miami, boss."

Darius sipped on his drink, making a disgusted face every time. "Maybe. I might head to New York, Paris, London, who knows. It's time for a vacation."

Eddie nodded. When Darius said he needed a vacation, that meant he needed time to clear his head and get ready for the next contract. He needed focus, precision. Taking contract after contract makes a man lose focus and becomes sloppy, and one thing Darius never was, was sloppy.

Eddie got up and walked out of the bar, leaving Darius to stare into the distance. He went over the details in his mind.

Alessandro Segreto. Tall, handsome, and too cocky in his own right. 6'1, built like a soccer player, dark green eyes and black hair. The Tagliatti family wanted him taken out nice and quiet, a silent warning to never touch the Don's daughter again. Not much tugged at Darius' heartstrings, but harming a woman and taking her against her will? That was an offense worthy of death in his eyes. But this mission wasn't harming a woman, merely a quick and gentle snatch to pull Alessandro out of hiding.

His phone pinged, the light of the phone almost shining through his dark glasses. A text from Eddie.

Name's Harmony. Cute little broad. Long black hair, Mediterranean complexion. Nice set of tits. Only one in town who can look like that in this hell hole. Entering in 5.

Darius looked up and locked eyes with the door. Eddie was right—a woman with that description, there couldn't be more than one in this shit town. He waited. The doorbell chimed and his ears were pierced with the twinkling sound of laughter. A crowd of women walked in, and there she was. Darius felt the breath knock out of him. Eddie must have left out some details; he didn't mention how gorgeous she was. Her long and silky, thick black hair cascaded around her small waist. Her thick legs and ass were so full he felt his cock starting to grow.

Down boy...business before pleasure.

His eyes followed her curves up to her large breasts hidden under a small, slinky plum dress. Her belly wasn't quite washboard flat, but it was very close. Her skin was glistening from a tan left over from the summer sun. Looking his way, he only caught a glimpse of blue eyes and a soft face. The gaggle of scantily clad women made their way to the bar and around the corner to a room offset from the main bar.

This was going to be a long night.

Chapter 2

Harmony

HARMONY CATRONE SAT off in a room opposite the bar. Once again, her sister was late meeting her at Kelly's Inn for their once-a-month bitch fest. She scrolled through TikTok on her phone, not looking up until she heard the door twinkle. Her long, thick, black hair was tied up in a tight bun and her thick, purple-rimmed glasses framed her face, the glare from the phone hiding the hurt in her blue eyes. She crossed her arms, eyeing the bar again. Callie came around the corner from the bar with another fuzzy navel in hand.

"Sofia late again?" She quipped.

Harmony let a small amount of air escape her lips. "Yeah. Again."

"I'm sorry, Harm. You wanna get some food while you wait? I'll put in an order for those pickles you like."

Harmony sighed. "I guess. Fuck waiting on her. I'm starving."

Callie leaned down close to her. "Hey. There's this really hot guy I've never seen before over in the corner booth near the kitchen. Says he's just passing through on his way to visit his grandmother. Maybe you should...you know..." Callie wiggled her hips and flicked back her blonde hair.

"Callie!"

"What? Just a thought. C'mon, girl, you're single, live a little. Plus, the guy looks *loaded*. Bet he'll buy you a drink."

With that Callie walked away and went back behind the bar.

Hot guy, huh?

The doorbell chimed and a man Harmony had never seen before walked past the doorway to the room and over in the direction of the kitchen. He had a well-oiled leather jacket and thick black hair, just like hers. Curiosity got the better of her and she got up to peek around the corner. He sat down at the booth Callie was talking about.

Holy fuck.

A man with broad shoulders and dark tinted glasses was slouched in the booth holding a small glass of what looked like whiskey. The white button-down shirt was perfectly pressed against his chest and the jeans almost left nothing to the imagination. What gave her almost instant wetness between her thighs was the mound of slicked-back orange hair that reminded her of a greaser in the '50s. She was a sucker for thicker men with wild hair colors. What really shook her senses was that fluffy, thick, ginger beard that could make any girl weak at the knees. He looked angry talking to the guy in the leather jacket, but she wasn't sure. She watched as Callie made her way over there with a beer and sat it on the table. She tried to get Callie's attention when she came back to the bar, but it was no use. The smoky haze was getting thicker, and she didn't want to draw attention to herself. She silently walked back to her booth where the waiting orange deliciousness was calling her name. There was next to no one in the back room except for a few of the local couples. She looked around, watching them. Some were cuddled up next to each other and others were having full on make-out sessions. It almost made her sick to her stomach watching them, a bout of jealousy rising in her throat. Thoughts of Gio started coming back to her, and she tried pushing them out of her mind. *Fucking asshole*, she thought. There was no way in hell the thought of Gio Velestra was going to upset her today. Not on *her* birthday. She looked again at the couples wishing she had a love like that. Why couldn't the man of her dreams just walk into the bar and sweep her off her feet? Especially a man like tall, dark, and ginger over there brooding in the corner. She couldn't help but think what it would be like to be in his arms and caressing her entire body, that stone look piercing through her making her nice and wet for his touch. *Stop it. Don't think about people like that.*

Why not, a husky voice whispered in the back of her mind. *He's certainly a meal I'd like to devour.* With her mind wandering and thinking about the ginger-stranger who sent her pussy into overdrive, she almost didn't hear the door chime again, but she certainly heard the obnoxious familiar laughter of Sofia and her friends. Harmony took a sip of her drink and watched her sister stumble back toward the room.

Look at her, she's a fucking mess.

The hyenas finally made it and Sofia almost fell into her seat at the booth.

"Harmony!" She squealed.

"You're late, Sofia." Harmony growled.

"C'mon, sis, don't be like that. I'm sorry but the girls wanted to come too. After all it's our birthday!"

Sofia squeezed her into a hug, and Harmony rolled her eyes. She pushed her twin sister off her. "Yeah, well, would've been nice if you didn't show up already shit faced."

Sofia blinked at her, her expression almost emotionless. "But, Harm, what fun is a birthday if you don't drink all day with the gals?"

Harmony sighed. "Look, Sof, I like drinking and partying as much as you, but you said this time it would be just you and me at our uncle's bar for a good birthday night out."

"Yeah...but...Angel and Tia really wanted to hang out to...day...*hiccup*...and Bella showed up...*hiccup*..."

Sofia could barely get her sentences out through her drunken hiccups. Angel and Tia piled in the booth, squishing Harmony almost out the seat. Their drunken laughter and screaming were already getting on her nerves. Callie came around the corner with her usual bottle of wine for the trio.

"So if Bella stopped by, where the hell is she at?"

Sofia hiccupped again. "She had to...*hiccup*...go home. She has a date with Gio."

Harmony turned stone white through her tanned skin. The bile rose in the throat, and she thought the fuzzy navels were going to come retching out of her mouth.

"The fuck did you just say?" Harmony spat.

"She's gonna go fuck Gio. Did...didn't I just say that?" Sofia giggled.

"Fuck you, Sofia. And your stupid fucking friends too."

"Oh shit...oh! I forgot, I'm sorry, Harm."

You didn't forget, you heartless bitch. You wanted me to know. Thanks a fucking lot.

Harmony got up from the booth. "I'm going home. You guys have fun or whatever."

"Harm, no, please stay."

Sofia tried to stand up to stop Harmony from leaving, but instead she fell forward knocking the open bottle of red wine to splash onto the table and splatter Harmony's matching plum dress.

Sofia stared at the red liquid flowing on the floor. "Fuck."

Harmony saw red, and it wasn't the wine. "What the *fuck*, Sofia! You've ruined my brand-new dress!"

"You can wear mine. Hold on." Sofia went to take her dress off, but Harmony slapped her hands and pulled them down to her side.

"Will you stop that! Are you fucking crazy?! You can't take your clothes off in the middle of the bar!"

"Oh, Harm..." Sofia started to let out the tears. "I ruined our matching birthday dresses..."

Jesus Cristo.

"C'mon."

Harmony grabbed Sofia's arm to pull her along, but Sofia stumbled again, falling into Harmony. Her hand reached out to stop herself, but Sofia, in her drunken haze, overshot and slammed her hand down on Harmony's bun, pulling it halfway out of the bun holder.

"SOFIA!" she screamed. Harmony immediately reached up to her ruined hair, feeling the throbbing pain of hair almost being ripped from her skull and the bobby pins jutting into her head.

"I'm sorry...I'm sorry..." Sofia kept repeating. This time, Harmony forcefully grabbed Sofia and dragged her into the women's bathroom next to their booth. Once inside, she locked the door.

"Fucking dammit, Sofia." Harmony screamed, turning back to her sister. "Can't you get ahold of yourself for once? You come in here late, a drunken mess, ruining our birthday like you *always* do. You only ever think about yourself and what *you* want. It's never about anyone else."

"Harm...that's not fair..."

"It *is* fair. This is just the straw that broke the camel's back."

Harmony turned away from her sister who looked like she wanted to cry again. *Let her.* Carefully, she pulled the bobby pins out of her hair and unrolled the bun shaper. Her long, curly black hair cascaded around her just like her sister's. With a Tide Pen in her purse and some soap and water from the sink, she tried to rub out the stain. Sofia stood there wobbling. She looked like one of those wacky inflatable waving tube men at the car dealership the way she was moving. With no desire for Sofia to rip out her hair again or take the time to put her bun back up, Harmony left her hair down. Harmony turned toward her sister. Her face looked like she wanted to hurl, but the only vomit that came out was her words.

"You're just mad Gio cheated on you and I have a loving man like Alessandro who would never do that to me."

As she spoke, Sofia's heel got caught in the grout between two tiles, lost her footing, and stumbled into Harmony...again. This time, Sofia wacked her in the face and sent her glasses flying only to break on the hard tile surface.

"Oh...." Sofia muttered.

Harmony was so pissed at Sofia's drunken ramblings that she kicked Sofia's legs out from under her with her stiletto pumps, knocking her to the ground. Sofia started to cry and scream from the pain of hitting the cold tiles. She ignored her, reaching down for her now broken glasses.

"Fucking had *enough* of you, Sofia." She gritted through her clenched jaw. The lenses were cracked, and the bridge of the nose busted in half. There was no fixing them. Luckily, Harmony dug inside of her purse and pulled out her spare set of contacts. Ignoring Sofia whining on the floor, she carefully placed the contacts on each eye with her manicured acrylic nails. She may not be the most beautiful woman in the world with her small fupa, professional hairstyle, and proper glasses, but she loved having her nails done. That was the one luxury she afforded herself to look and feel beautiful other than some of her clothes.

Blinking, her blurred version went to sharp and in focus. Looking down, she realized Sofia had stopped her incessant whining. Sofia was passed out on the floor.

Ugh...

Reaching down, Harmony pulled her sister up and flung her so she could get an arm underneath her to support her back. Unlocking the door, she half-dragged Sofia out to the table where Tia and Angel were still laughing and carrying on with a new bottle of wine. Callie must have put it on the table while they were in the bathroom. The wine was gone from the floor and table, almost like it was never there. Harmony threw Sofia into the booth on top of Angel and Tia.

"Take her the fuck home. Let Alessandro deal with her ass."

She turned on her heel and stomped out of the room. Without looking, she waved to Callie that she was leaving. She doubted she was able to see her through all the cigar and cigarette smoke. Throwing the door to the bar open, she took a deep breath of the warm night air. The smell of pine trees and hot asphalt was more comforting than the stale smoke. She tried to not let her tears escape her eyes as she walked to her car around the back of the building. As she reached for the door handle, she felt like something was wrong. The hair on the back of her neck stood up, and her gut told her to hurry and get in the car. Pulling the door open, she felt the sharp sting of something snake around her throat and a growing pressure causing her to choke. Grabbing up at her throat, she felt the familiar feel of a man's arm. Another arm, clad in a white long sleeve, placed a rag around her mouth as she tried to scream. The only thing she could make out was there was a music note cufflink where the normal button would be.

It was just like in the movies. Slowly, everything went black.

Darius

DARIUS' TARGET WALKED right past him into the back room behind the bar. He had to sharpen up and not let his cock lead the way. He wanted nothing more than to throw her down on his custom silk sheets and fuck her until she came around his cock and he himself climax deep inside her. But that wasn't what this mission was for. This wasn't a one-night stand mission with yet another unknown broad—this was business. He could hear yelling in the back, then the slam of a bottle. The bartender was going back and forth from the room to the bar, and he could tell by her expression the party was upsetting her. Classic sign along with the yelling that soon they would be leaving. He gulped the last of his cheap whiskey and placed a $100 bill on the table. Slinking out of the booth, he silently made his way outside. He walked around the side of the building away from the street-lights. In the shadows across the parking lot, he had a perfect view of the door. It wasn't long until the door burst open, and there she was, stomping with fury around the side of the building to her car. The fury in her body only aroused him more.

He slunk from the shadows and slithered around the cars, watching her every move. She stood at her car, fumbling for her keys. This was the moment to pounce. Without a sound, he crept up behind her and took the chloroform rag out of his pants pocket. Swift as ever, he snaked his arm around her throat and pulled her toward him. She went to scream, but he had already moved in and placed the rag over her face. Instantly, she was limp in his arms. Scooping her up, his hands graced her ass as he pulled her up into his body. He felt his own body pulse and ache for her touch, and he had to remind himself of his own rules. He could not take this woman against her will, no matter how much he wanted inside of her.

He walked around the side of the car and opened the passenger door, placing her in the seat. He slammed the door shut and walked back around with her keys and climbed into the driver's seat. Starting up the used Genesis, they left as silently as he nabbed her. Driving along the road to his safe house, he quickly pulled out his phone and called Eddie.

"Eddie. Got her. Prepare her room."

Eddie didn't even get a chance to say anything before Darius hung up.

The same smirk played across his lips. *Time to come out and play, Alessandro...*

Harmony

WHERE AM I?

Through blurred vision, Harmony could just make out she was in a room on a bed. Her head was pounding and foggy.

What happened? How did I get in bed?

She tried to think back and remembered fighting with Sofia. There was the spilled wine, the stain on her dress, the fight in the bathroom, and the last thing she remembered was walking out to her car. So how did she get here?

Her vision started to clear. She realized she wasn't in her own room. It had a large canopy bed complete with black silk sheets. The set of windows and a sliding glass door led out to a large balcony with a comfy deck chair and a table with an umbrella. Narrowing her eyes, she could tell there was an alarm attached to both the door and the windows and a row of small red laser lights went across the glass. An ornate oak desk was in one corner of the room. The desk had a basket of fruit with apples, grapes, and oranges. On the other side of the room was a small baker's rack complete with tea and coffee cups and the largest variety of tea and coffee she had ever seen. Looking around the room she could tell she was in a mansion—the room was four times the size of her own apartment. A velvet, antique Victorian couch and chair were off to the side of the room by the bed facing the door. An 80-inch TV was placed on the wall in front of her.

OK…well I'm in a mansion. But what the fuck am I doing in the mansion?

She got up out of the bed and walked over to the desk. Looking down, she realized she wasn't in her dress. Instead, she was clad in a soft silk nightgown that barely went down to her thighs and had a high lace slit up the side.

I didn't even wear this nightgown yet; I just bought it… Did I go home first?

While chowing down on an apple, the juice dripping down her chin, a soft knock came at the door. Before she could answer, the door opened. There in the doorway stood the man from the bar. She immediately felt the pressure grow inside her and the pulsating of her pussy was enough to make her drip between her legs. He stood there, watching her, leaning up against the doorway with one arm resting on the trim above him. He walked in, closing the door behind him. Yet again, his vibrant orange hair was slicked back, his white crisp silk shirt was perfectly tailored to his broad chest, and his purple dress pants she wished would show more than what it was offering. She caught herself staring at the zipper of his pants and turned her gaze away. She wanted to keep looking and give this man her famous temper that sent everyone else running and groveling at her feet. But for some reason, she also wanted to be on her knees in front of him, for more than one reason.

"I see you're awake, *mia curore.*"

Harmony felt her cheeks grow hot. Did he just call her his heart?

She wanted him badly, but she had to stay strong and find out why she was here and what he wanted with her.

"Where did you take me? What do you want with me?" She crossed her arms over her chest, the coolness of the room forcing her nipples to peak and push against the silk of her nightgown.

He gestured to the bed. "Sit, and I will tell you."

Harmony walked over with apple still in hand to the bed and sat on the edge.

"Talk."

Behind the white shaded glasses that hid his eyes, an orange eyebrow raised over the rim.

"I wouldn't be the one making demands if I was you."

He walked over and pulled out the chair by the desk, turning it around and straddling it. Harmony had to shift in her spot to prevent the wetness from escaping.

"I'm not one to beat around the bush. I don't do the mysterious bullshit of playing games when it comes to business. You're here because I need to find your boyfriend. I have you, he'll come out, and I'll kill him."

Harmony stared at him. Was he *serious* right now? She couldn't help but begin to laugh.

"And what boyfriend would that be? Look if you want Gio I'll lead you right to him the bastard, slit his throat, tie him to a car or a brick and toss him in the sea. I don't care whatever you do to him; he deserves it."

She couldn't see his expression behind the glasses, but she could tell she derailed whatever his plans were.

"Gio?" he said softly.

"Yes, Gio. I don't know why you want him, but you can have him."

All he did was smile.

"Where are my manners? I never introduced myself. My name is Darius."

Harmony cocked her head. "Harmony."

Darius swung his leg from around the chair and walked to the door. "Plans may have changed for you, *mia curore*. We'll talk soon."

Before he walked out, he peeked back around the door. "And I wouldn't try to open any of the windows and doors. Your room is being monitored."

Darius left, locking the door behind him.

Darius

IMMEDIATELY, DARIUS stormed down the hall and up the extra set of stars to his office. His polished oxford saddle shoes clacked against the dark-stained hardwood oak floors. Taking out his keys and opening the locked door to his office, he slammed it shut behind him. He walked over to his desk and pulled out his file. Photos of Harmony and Alessandro graced the pages, but something ate away at him. Why did she mention this Gio person and not Alessandro? Was that his nickname?

He picked up his phone and dialed Eddie.

"Yes, boss?"

"What the fuck did you do?"

"Drank, smoke, possibly fucked this broad I met last night, why? You need a girl?"

"No, you fucking idiot. I want to know why you gave me the wrong information."

The phone went silent for a moment. *"I did my job."*

"You're slipping."

"She matches the description and all the photos."

Darius stared at them...hard.

"Wait a fucking minute..."

Darius picked up the photo of Harmony and Alessandro at a nearby small-town night club. He noticed there were no tattoos on her. The woman he had in his guest room had a small pawprint on her arm and he saw a glimpse of a thigh piece.

"Eddie."

"What?"

"The woman in the photos doesn't have any tattoos. This Harmony I have in my guest room has at least two of them."

"...*Fuck*."

"I'm calling Ramiro. We're getting this settled *now*."

Darius slammed his desk phone down and picked up his cell. He pressed two buttons, and the phone didn't even ring.

"Yes, sir."

"Alessandro Segreto. Find him. Eddie fucked up. Who's the girl?"

The phone was silent for all of 5 seconds before Ramiro had the information he needed.

"Sorry, sir. His girl is Sofia Catrone. Family owns a couple of businesses in the area. Construction, bars."

"Anyone named Harmony?"

Ramiro was silent again for a moment. "Sister. Harmony Catrone. Twin."

Darius' eyes went wide.

"Thank you, Ramiro. I'll have your pay in a few minutes."

"Thank you, sir."

Darius hung up and ran his fingers through his hair. He knew he shouldn't have given Eddie another chance. He'd been slipping, and he dropped the ball yet again. In this line of business, mistakes like this couldn't happen. He'd be punished properly, and Ramiro would be his go-to for information from now on. Eddie was a liability, and liabilities are to be...settled.

This changed everything.

This wasn't Alessandro's girlfriend, but rather the girlfriend's sister. If his intelligence was correct, Alessandro wouldn't give a fuck about her unless Sofia demanded that he do something about it. He didn't know much about her to know if she would be upset if her sister went missing. He had to find out what happened last night and asking her seemed like the best bet. That smile curved again at the corner of his mouth. She was single. And he noticed earlier that she turned his cock harder than the night before. His morals be damned. He would have Harmony and make her like what he had to offer.

Harmony

SHE COULDN'T BELIEVE he just left her there! And what was that about not escaping? And who the hell would want Gio dead anyway? *Well, that's a stupid question to ask. I do.* She already finished her apple and started getting to work on the grapes. She explored the room, seeing that many of her clothes were in the closet. She needed more answers than what he gave her, and she'd get them. Harmony walked over to her purse sitting on the desk and pulled out some cream, squeezing it on her palms and rubbing it on her body, especially her tattoos. She paid good money for them and always wanted them at their finest. She rubbed the cream over her shoulder, gently rubbing it over the pawprint tattoo. She then lifted her leg up onto the chair Darius had sat on and pulled up her nightgown slightly, fully exposing her thigh. A garter belt tattoo encircled her leg, red lace with a classic Sailor Moon locket in the center and charms hanging down from the garter. She smiled. Harmony was a sucker for anime, and Sailor Moon was one of her favorites growing up.

After applying the lotion, she pulled the nightgown back down and walked over to the bed. She could see a door slightly ajar off to the side of the bed. Peeking in, she found a large master bathroom complete with a separate shower and clawfoot tub. Towels were stacked on a built-in shelf. Soaps and lotions—brands she could never dream of owning—were stacked in a cabinet next to the shower. The large walk-in shower featured a waterfall over jutting rocks and a showerhead that was built into the ceiling, covering the pebbled ground behind the glass wall. The huge clawfoot tub was marbled with Victorian-style fixings. Next to the tub was a variety of candles and bath-bombs. Looking up, she saw another sliding glass door leading out to another balcony. On the balcony was a jacuzzi.

"I wasn't sure what all you'd like, so I got a little of everything."

Harmony jumped at the sound of the liquid voice that soothed and caressed like Neil Patrick Harris but had perfect Robert De Niro grit. She was so enthralled by the gorgeous bathroom that she hadn't heard the lock click on the door and Darius come into the room. She quickly turned around and saw him leaning up against the bathroom doorway.

"I'm sorry...it's just so gorgeous!"

He slowly stepped inside.

"If there's anything you need, let me know and I'll get you anything you want."

Why the hell was this god of a man being so nice to her? Harmony stamped her foot down and crossed her arms.

"I need to know why *else* I'm here. You can't tell me you kidnapped me just to pull Gio out of hiding. The man doesn't hide, and you don't need me."

Darius looked away then looked back into her eyes. "It seems as though my assistant made a mistake. The man I'm after is Alessandro."

Harmony couldn't believe what she was hearing. She wasn't surprised that disgusting fucker had gotten into some trouble. "My sister's boyfriend?"

"Yes."

Now she was angry. She was angry that Sofia ever got into a relationship with that creep in the first place. She warned her about fucking him, and now look. Once again Sofia and her stupidity got her into a mess.

Harmony huffed and threw her arms. "This is just fucking great."

"I understand you're upset..."

Harmony held up her hand and cut Darius off. "It's not *you*. It's this whole situation. My sister constantly fucks up her life *and* mine because she lacks enough cognitive development to do anything right."

She wanted to let the hot tears flow down her face, but she was stronger than that. And she certainly wasn't going to look vulnerable in front of him. Quickly wiping her eyes, she looked back up at him.

"What did he do that you want to kill him?"

"Simple. He harmed a Don's daughter. Raped her."

Suddenly, it clicked. He was a master *sicario*.

"Who do you work for?"

"No one."

He was quick to answer.

"It was Paola Tagliatti, wasn't it?"

Darius stood silent, watching her.

"Yes," he finally admitted.

Harmony shook her head. "Fucking knew it."

"Care to share?" He quipped.

Harmony looked away, tapping her foot. She didn't know if she should be telling Darius all of this, but something in her Sicilian gut told her it was the right thing.

"I don't know anything outside of what my sister mentioned. The son of a bitch mentioned to her a few times if she didn't 'act right', he'd do to her like he did Paola. Funny enough, Paola is an old friend from college. We met in our freshman year. She called me the night he raped her."

Darius stood listening to her story about how Paola begged her to come to Chicago to stay with her and help her tell her father. She was very close with Don Tagliatti, he even saw her as his adopted daughter.

"When Sofia got involved with him, I didn't know it was the same person. Not until he mentioned Paola, and I called her up, asking her that *cazzo's* name. She told me it was Alessandro, my sister's new boyfriend. I tried to get her to leave him, telling her he was no good. She didn't listen. She doesn't know he's been cheating on her, and I see the bruises he leaves on her."

Darius lowered his eyes. "I'm sorry you got mixed up in this."

Harmony waved her hand. "It's done."

Harmony watched as he stood for a moment, then turned to walk away.

"Darius." She called.

He turned back around to face her.

"What if I help you find him?"

Darius

DID SHE JUST OFFER to help him? In all the years he'd been a hired hit man for the mafia around the world, not once had someone involved with the victim offer to help him. There was more to this woman than he knew, and he wanted to explore every bit of it.

"Do you really want to help? You don't understand the work I'm in."

Harmony stepped closer to him, the little negligee leaving nothing to the imagination as to what was beneath it. He felt his cock grow and it ached against his Versace custom dress pants. He had to remain strong, no matter how much he wanted to unleash it and show her a good time. He sucked in his breath as she was only inches from him. He had to change the subject, fast.

"Who is this Gio you were talking about?"

She stopped in her tracks and looked away. "He's my ex. He decided that multiple women was more his style...and he's not poly."

Darius felt his blood boiling. Who would ever harm this perfect deity? What sick, twisted, demented fuck would cheat on this delicate rose? Once the business with Alessandro was done, he wanted to take care of this Gio himself, with or without a contract. He could tell by the way she spoke and her manners in the little time of knowing her that she was not only beautiful, but there was a soft and caring side. The way she spoke about Gio and Alessandro proved this rose had thorns.

"Mia rosa." He whispered.

"What was that?"

"You." He didn't know what possessed him to do it, but he gently took her hand in his. It was creamy, the feel of cashmere. He clasped her hand in his. "You are a rose. It's my job to read people. I can see you have a caring heart until someone hurts you, then you pull out the thorns."

Harmony smiled. "That's what my mother always says."

Darius gently lifted her hand to his lips. "You're still willing to help even after my mistake, *mia rosa*?"

Harmony smiled so wickedly, he wanted to take her right there on the bathroom floor.

"Absolutely."

Harmony

FOR SOME REASON, AGREEING to help Darius felt so right. Sofia had fucked with her life enough, and if this was the way to teach her sister a lesson to wise-up then so be it. She lay on the bed, caressing her hand against her chest. After their conversation in the bathroom, Darius told her to meet him later for dinner downstairs. When he left, he didn't lock the door and all the alarms mysteriously disappeared from the windows while she showered. She kept thinking about how he sounded, how good his touch felt. There was something about him she couldn't place. She only just met him, but he made her feel safe and loved. She never felt this way around any of her boyfriends, not even Gio. Sexually, she wanted him badly. She wanted him underneath her, moaning her name, begging to touch her, her pussy squeezing his cock and milking it dry until he couldn't come anymore.

She felt herself grow hot, pulsating, waiting for her treat. She sobered up out of her lustful thoughts when she thought, *Does he feel the same way about me?*

It wasn't fair to think he wanted her just as badly. Except it wasn't hard to see he had some sort of attraction to her the way he shifted and allowed his cock to try and play peek-a-boo under his pants.

She had to find out. Harmony Catrone was no damsel-in-distress. She didn't even care that he kidnapped her at this point, now knowing the full story. Everything started to click. She was a woman who took what she wanted when she wanted it, and Darius would be no different.

Darius

DARIUS WALKED AROUND the dining room table, making sure everything was perfect. An Italian like himself...well...half Italian...he couldn't see her turning down a perfectly cooked meal of meatballs, pollo alla cacciatora, caprese pasta, and finish it out with freshly made tiramisu and cannolis by his Sicilian chef. After lighting the red taper candles, he grabbed the wine bottle that Stefano pulled out for him from the wine cellar off the table. Grabbing the corkscrew, he expertly twisted it into the cork and the familiar *pop* was music to his ears. He wafted in the smell from the open neck of the 1945 Brunello di Montalcino. Perfection. He thought about going up to knock on her door to tell her dinner was ready, but there was no need. He heard the clack of heels against the hardwood stairs. Darius looked up and watched as the vision in red took delicate steps down each stair. The heels were black and strappy, and the bodycon dress held her curves snug. Her little fupa at her stomach and thick thighs took his breath and gave him a raging hard-on in return. It glittered under the soft candlelight. The dress had a long slit up the side of her right leg, exposing her thigh. He could tell she wasn't wearing any panties or a bra for that matter. Her nipples poked at the thin fabric and her long hair cascaded down her back. He walked over to the other chair and pulled it out for her. She smiled and sat delicately as he pushed it in toward the table.

Harmony eyed up the spread. "Mmmm, pollo alla cacciatora. My favorite."

Darius grabbed the wine bottle and poured the red liquid into her glass. "Really?" he said curiously. *I'll have to thank Ramiro later for that information.*

She took the tongs and scooped some caprese pasta to start out with. He sat down on the other side of the small table. He was thankful he took out the 6 leaves earlier that made it from a table that could fit 15 to a more intimate setting. They eyed each other as they ate and sipped wine.

"Why did you decide to become a hit man?"

Darius was never taken by surprise, but her question caught him off guard and almost made him spit out his wine.

"Excuse me?"

"A *maestro sicario.* Why?"

She continued eating forkfuls of pasta, barely batting an eye like her question was polite conversation. He loved a woman who got right to the point.

Darius shrugged his shoulders. "Money. Prestige. And I just like whacking people."

"Just people who deserve it or anyone?"

"I don't normally let people into my business, *mia rosa*. But if you must know, it doesn't matter to me. I ice anybody the money tells me to. Makes no difference who or why."

Darius watched as her eyes flared and a small curl tease at her lips.

She was enjoying this.

They continued eating, making actual polite conversation. The bottle of wine quickly disappeared and by the time they hit the cannolis, tiramisu, and coffee, they were giggling and smiling.

"You mean to tell me you're the one who put Luca Rosso in the meat freezer and set The Batello on fire with its own liquor?" Harmony spat through fits of giggles.

Darius laughed with her. "That's right. Luca didn't know what was comin'. The *capo* with Don Marcano said he was tired of Luca acting like a pig in his nightclub and skimming the till. So, I only treated him the way he acted and set The Batello on fire so they could claim insurance losses. Surprised the fucker stayed frozen after it burnt down. I was hoping he'd make some crispy bacon."

They laughed heartily until Harmony went to reach for the wine bottle and tried pouring the empty bottle into her glass.

"Would you like another?" he asked.

She nodded in approval. Darius walked around to her side of the table and picked up her hand, placing it once again against his lips. "Be right back, *mia rosa*."

She watched as he walked away to a door near the stairs and opened it, going down below.

Harmony stared at the room. Looking over toward the front door by the foyer, she saw a large living room. In the room there were comfortable leather couches and chairs. A large ceiling to floor bay of windows, bookcases lined with books of all genres from smutty to Shakespeare. By the window was a large grand piano. She smiled as she walked toward the piano.

DARIUS WALKED DOWN the steps into the wine cellar. Looking through the catacomb of hundreds of bottles, he found the one he was looking for. He pulled out the bottle off the rack and blew off the dust. *The 1907 Shipwrecked Heidsieck will do.* Above him, he heard a strange sound. He'd left the door ajar and realized the sound he was hearing was melodic and soothing. It was the piano in the grand parlor. The tone tugged at his heart, making him feel calmer than he had been in many years. He felt himself giving in to the notes. Who was playing that beautiful music?

He gently walked back up the stairs with the wine in hand. Coming around the corner and walking the few steps to the door of the parlor, he peeked in and saw Harmony sitting on the bench at the keys. Listening more intently, he realized she was playing the Moonlight Sonata.

Darius wasn't sure but it felt like his jaw dropped. She was already everything he had ever dreamed of, and this was icing on the cake. A woman who adored classical music? He didn't want to ruin the moment, watching her play from a distance, her body swaying to the resonating sound of hammers hitting strings.

He silently walked up to her beside the piano. "Beethoven. I'm impressed."

Harmony looked up at him but continued to play. "You know it?"

Darius leaned against the piano. "Of course I do. Beethoven was a favorite growing up, although one of my favorite pieces is his Symphony number nine in D minor."

Harmony stopped. "That was the one piece I could never master. Can you play it for me?"

Darius smiled. "Of course."

They switched places and she stood behind him as he warmed up his fingers. He began to play. They both gave in to the music, closing their eyes and becoming drunk on the notes. She leaned in close, her body pressing against his back. Her arm snaked around his chest as she pushed her full breasts into him. They both sharply inhaled. His fingers began to fumble as her mouth came close to his ear.

"Darius?" She whispered.

"Yes?" He barely choked out.

"I need to know something. I saw what happened in the bathroom. And I could tell the moment you looked at me walking down the stairs. Do you want me?"

What the hell. He stopped, turning toward her. His arm quickly wrapped around her and pulled her in so forcefully her mouth was barely touching his. He realized he was still wearing his protective glasses so she couldn't see his eyes. She had no idea the heat that was burning inside, poisoning him.

"I've wanted you since the moment I saw you."

That was all she needed to hear. Her mouth went down on his, her hands curling through his hair. She moaned against his lips and he felt his cock stand at immediate attention. This was it. She was about to be his.

Harmony

SHE GOT WHAT SHE WANTED. She didn't think it would take playing the piano to finally have his cock, but that didn't matter. She was tired of her pussy begging for relief, her swollen lips crying for an orgasm. His words were music to her ears, and that was her cue to make the move. Harmony was never one to play games and hard to get if she didn't have to. This man turned her on so badly she wasn't waiting for him to take her. His sweet talk and the well-tailored black suit, white shirt with the silken green tie, were enough to make her want to come right there on the stairs when she walked down. Thanks to the slit in her dress, she found herself easily able to straddle him. She felt his hands graze over her ass and grab hard. She moaned against his lips. Nothing else mattered right now. Not Alessandro, not Sofia—all that mattered was having him inside her.

She did this on purpose, and it was working beautifully. Her fingers curled in in his hair, pushing his mouth harder on hers. They both parted their lips at the same time and began to explore each other's mouths with their tongues. His scent, his taste, it enflamed her. He picked her up and swung her around to place her on the piano lid. She almost felt sorry for it, but he didn't seem to care that he almost broke the lid prop by slamming her down onto the hard wood. His hands expertly worked his way down her neck and cupped her breasts. He pulled one out, exposing it in all its glory. Darius's hot kisses left a trail of fire from her lips to her neck and down to her nipple where he began to lick and suck on it so gently that she wanted to arch her back and push his mouth on it harder. His tongue continued to dance and tease, perking up her nipple. She didn't even feel it when he pulled out the other one and began to tweak the nubbed flesh between his fingers. She writhed in his hands, unable to control the growing pressure and heat between her legs. He made his way down and spread her legs open. She was wet, pink, and ready. Both sets of lips begged him to take her. He grabbed her thighs, pulling her closer to his mouth. She almost screamed when his tongue delved into her pussy. He lapped at her juices, guttural moans escaping her throat. She felt herself grabbing his head and pushing him in deeper, and he responded by working his hands under her ass and pulling her into him even more. His tongue flicked inside her pink walls, playing with her pierced clit. One hand worked its way out and began to rub right where her piercing was while he continued to eat her out. She couldn't stand it anymore. She was so close to the verge of her own orgasm, but he stopped right when she was about to reach her peak.

She looked down and saw him looking up at her. Standing up, she could see how hard his cock was. She licked her lips, wanting to taste him like he tasted her. She had to hold back the animal inside her that wanted to rip those expensive dress pants open and let his cock spring forth in all its magnificence. Darius picked her up by her waist like she was nothing but a feather to him. He positioned her to wrap her legs around him so he could walk them over to the large Victorian couch with gold inlays over by the bank of bay windows. He tossed her down onto the black velvet. He stood up, his hands reaching down to unbutton his pants.

"Wait." Her voice was raspy, almost a whisper.

He stopped. She maneuvered herself up and reached for him. Her manicured nails slithered past the silk trim of the waist band, her thumb flicking his belt apart. If there was one thing she was an expert at, it was getting a man's pants to the ground. She undid the buckle and popped the buttons, her hands sliding the black cloth down past his thighs until they dropped to the floor.

Well, hello there...

Turns out she wasn't the only one expecting to get fucked tonight, since there it was staring back at her, a glorious, unsheathed sword hard and ready for action. Harmony had seen plenty of different cocks in her life, in more ways than one. But this one...it was the most beautiful thing she ever saw. It was long, hard, and perfectly thick. And would you look at that...the carpet matches the drapes. Gently, she wrapped her fingers around the shaft. Already it was pulsing beneath her hand, and she heard Darius moan a sigh of relief. She didn't want this moment to end, so she slowly started stroking it, her mouth leaning in to suck on his head. Her tongue flicked over his skin, cradling it as her hand moved up and down his shaft. He reached to put his hand on the back of her head.

"Suck it." His voice had changed from the soft and gritty undertones she was used to, to demanding and cold. The change stirred something inside her she didn't understand. She felt him grip her hair and pull it downwards, so she had to raise her chin to face him. He was looking down at her.

"I want that mouth, *mia rosa. Now.*"

Yes, daddy!

He released his grip only slightly so she could reposition her head before she took his full shaft in her mouth. Her tongue going over every part she could possibly reach. She cupped his balls, her fingers dancing closely between them and his ass. The sound he made was primeval, instinctive. He wrapped his fingers in her hair, pushing her to help her. He tasted divine, like a heady mix of desire and bourbon-laced bodywash. Tears started to flow down her cheeks. Never in her life had she wanted a man so badly it caused her to cry. She wanted to please him, to have him come in her mouth so deep it would hit the back of her throat. He must have known what she wanted since he started to thrust his hips faster and faster until he cried out, holding her tight against him. Harmony responded by pulling him in as hard as she could, letting the salty liquid drip down her tongue into her throat. She felt a sense of euphoria feeling him squirt so hard it hit with such force at the back of her throat, and she gladly swallowed every, last drop.

Why does this feel so good? Please, Darius, give me more. Don't let this end...

Pulling his cock out of her mouth, she looked up to see him smiling.

"That won't do, *mia rosa*. I'm not done with you yet."

He was so quick that she was almost instantaneously on her back on the couch. She looked down to see nothing had changed, he was still rock hard. It almost looked like he was even harder than he was before he came. Taking off his jacket and unbuttoning his shirt, he revealed a broad chest with the beginnings of a small 6-pack. She reached up to run her fingers down his chest and followed the little orange trail down to his cock.

Harmony felt a shiver of anticipation go down her spine. She didn't know what he was going to do to her, but he hoped he would bring her some relief and fast.

"What do you want from me, Darius?"

He leaned in close to her. "I thought that was obvious." He leaned even closer until his lips grazed her left ear. "*You.*"

The moment he said it, she felt him enter her. The feeling of him filling her almost made her explode on the spot. Her mind swirled, the ecstasy too much for her to handle. Waves of pleasure washed over her as he pumped inside her. Something in her mind clicked. Decades of tampered-down feelings and pain and hurt came boiling up. He was the key to unlocking her true potential. Tears poured out of her eyes, letting the feeling take her where she needed to go. He watched her every move, realizing what was happening. For the first time, he reached up and took his glasses off his face, never breaking his stride. Harmony stared back into deep black pools. Most women would be turned off by a man who had black eyes, but she found it sexy as hell.

No wonder he kept them hidden behind those glasses...

A new world opened to her. She saw lust, desire, and aching need... for her inside his eyes. She wrapped her arms around him, letting a guttural moan escape her lips as she reached her peak and the tears kept coming of pure pleasure.

"Darius..." she cried, her voice pained with an aching need. Their eyes were locked, and neither one of them were going to look away as they came together.

He thrust deep inside her, both of them coming and orgasming, their bodily fluids mixing together in peaceful harmony.

"Harmony..." he whispered as they climaxed together. She felt his body, slick with sweat, grow tense in her arms then limp as he spent his energy into her.

Harmony felt her soul leave her body. It almost pained her to feel him pull his cock out of her, but he only got up long enough to walk over to a large oak chest by a closet door and pull out a thick sherpa blanket. The couch was large enough to comfortably fit the both of them, so she slid over a little as he went to lie on the couch beside her, holding her close to his chest. Harmony wrapped one arm around him, lying her head on his heavily beating chest after quickly landing a soft kiss on his neck. Darius looked down and gently kissed her on the lips. She wanted more of his lips, but her body was too much like Jell-O lying between him and the arched back of the couch. Both perfectly content, he pulled the blanket over them, and they sat drinking in each other's company, letting the moment take them. Soon, she drifted off to sleep.

Chapter 6

Darius

WHAT THE FUCK WAS HIS life coming to? Within the last two days everything was turned upside down. He went from business and doing a typical hit to having a woman freely walk about his mansion sending his cock into spasms every time he looked at her like he was a horny teenager. For the first time, sex didn't feel like a biological need he had to release...it felt like home. He didn't know how to love them, to give them what they needed besides sexual satisfaction. Darius had always kept love and sex separate. Was it really supposed to be? He used them, fucked their brains out, then moved on to the next one, never getting attached because of his line of work. But this one...she *wanted* in. Since last night, he felt his heart *and* his cock aching to please her. He wanted to see her smile, to bring her into every-thing about his life. He'd already told her more than he probably should have, and she took it in, even giving suggestions on how to pull Alessandro out of hiding. It was like she was meant to be in this world, to be his. Everything was going so fast he could hardly contain it. The dinner, the ease of talking about his work, her willingness to help him find Alessandro and bring him down, the delightful and sublime sex...he was *enjoying* it. The worst part was, he didn't know if it was a good thing or a mistake. Villains weren't supposed to get a happy ending.

Today, Darius was going over his plans in his study when she waltzed in. No woman had ever been in his office, but there she was, clad in one of his button-down shirts and lace-topped panties with a messy bun standing in his doorway. His cock immediately raised the flagpole, saluting her. His imagination started to run with it, thinking about ripping open those buttons, exposing her naked breasts underneath, grabbing her and nailing her right there on his desk. He couldn't decide what was sexier...the red dress last night or this laid-back don't-give-a-fuck look. He had to control himself. Last night he was able to let himself go, to give his all to her. Today was business. If he spent all his time fucking her, he'd never get any work done. No work meant no money, which meant no treating her to the lifestyle she deserved. That thought sobered him up only slightly.

She strutted across the lush, carpeted floor, the only room in the house except his bedroom with carpet flooring. Harmony came around the desk and hoisted herself up, popping her ass right on the wood. She looked down at the papers in front of him. It was too late to hide them now. She thumbed through them, acting like he wasn't even there. *Cheeky cunt.*

Suddenly, she spoke. "That's your problem, you're doing this wrong."

Darius raised an eyebrow. "Excuse me?"

"Here..." she shuffled a few papers across the desk. "I've been around the bastard long enough to figure out his kind. If a woman is willing to open her legs to him, he's on it like a *cagna* in heat." She smiled that wicked smile that had Darius like putty in her hands. "I don't really think he's in love with my sister. They met in Miami when she was down there over the summer with Paola."

Darius held up a hand and stopped her. "Your sister was in Miami with Paola?"

Harmony rolled her eyes. "Yes, pay attention Darius. *Papà* Tagliatti offered to have us go down there for the whole summer as a graduation gift since the three of us just got done with our master's degrees. I stayed home, but they went, and she found him in a nightclub. The three of them have been inseparable ever since. When they had to go home, he followed. Paola told me the story of how he raped her the night before they left. She never told my sister about it; she was so scared and embarrassed. After she called me and told me, I begged her to tell *Papà* Tagliatti. Took her a week to get the courage to tell him. And here we are."

Darius sat back in his chair and folded his arms. His purple sweatpants and white T-shirt showing her his every curve. He enjoyed being comfortable in his own office, and she looked just as comfortable in his shirt.

"Then tell me, *mia rosa*, how am I going about this 'all wrong'? And why didn't you go with them?"

Harmony looked away from him. "I needed a job. Wanted to make money to help pay for my parents' house in foreclosure. They lost a lot of money by constantly bailing my sister out of her stupid decisions and sending us both to college. So, I asked *Papà*

Tagliatti if there was anything I could do. I've been his best *capo* ever since."

Darius's eyes grew wide, and this time, he didn't have his glasses on to hide his expression from her.

"You..."

Harmony smiled. "Yes, me. I was the one who convinced him to put the hit out on Alessandro. I didn't know you'd accidentally kidnap me in the process."

Everything started to fall into place. She was already mixed up in this world. That's why she was so willing to help him and wasn't afraid when he nabbed her. She knew who he was the entire time.

"I know that look." Her voice cut through his thoughts. "I didn't know you were the one he hired that night in the bar. All he told me was he hired the best in the world to take care of the problem. I didn't figure it out until you told me you were looking for Alessandro."

His heart jumped from his chest to his stomach, up to his throat and back again. The thought crossed his mind that she may have used this to spy on him, use him. The experience they shared last night was enough to prove that theory false.

She reached out and placed her hand under his chin. No one else would have even been able to walk into the office, let alone touch him. It was a testament to prove just how much he trusted her. "I want him *morta,* Darius. And I need your help."

He grabbed her hand and moved it from under his chin to his lips, kissing the lusciously soft skin. Her golden rings set with diamonds and rubies glittered from the sunlight streaming in through the window. "Any other man would think you were using him with that admission, *mia rosa.*"

Harmony cast her eyes downward. "I'm sorry. I never wanted you to think that. I...I'm not..."

He saw her trying to keep the tears from escaping her eyes. He stood up, pulling her off the desk and into his arms. Every fiber of his being wanted to take whatever pain she was feeling away from her.

He didn't know what to do except to just be there for her and let her feel whatever it was she was feeling.

"Let it out, *mia rosa*."

"Everything's happening so fast. One minute I'm back home keeping tabs on him and my sister and the next I'm in your home having mind-blowing sex that I never thought I could feel."

You and me both...

Darius gently lifted her chin up to face him. "Tell me."

Harmony let out a rattled sigh. "All my life I've had horrible boyfriends, lovers, whatever. They only wanted one thing from me. I was seen as a trophy, a toy to play with. No one except my parents, *Papà* Tagliatti, and Paola respected me. I'm sorry to dump all this on you. I know we've only been together one night but...I feel like you respect me. You understand me. Darius, you're nothing like all those other guys. I don't give a damn what you do, because I'm in that world. That is my life now. This is gonna sound crazy but..." He could barely hear her when she whispered, "I want to live in our world with you."

Her admission was a smack in the face. All night lying with her in his arms he had thought about the same thing. It didn't matter that it had been one day, one night. There was a connection there he couldn't explain. Whatever that connection was, he wasn't going to break it. And he'd go to hell and back and do whatever it takes to keep her in his life as his permanent lover...and hopefully more.

The heat rose in his body, revealing itself in his dark eyes. As he looked into her blue pools, they ached for him to respond. He pressed his lips hard on hers, delving into her mouth. She melted in his arms, responding with her tongue and an urge that matched his own. He broke away from her, leaving her in a daze.

"You are *mine, mia rosa.* And *no one* will ever take you away from me." He growled.

She smiled, teasing him. "And what would you do for me?"

Darius returned the smile. He didn't know what possessed him to do it, but the sharp Bowie knife came sliding out of its holster and he held it in his hand. The wrapped leather and long stainless-steel blade felt like an extension of his own arm. He brandished it in front of her, the steel glittering from the sun. Her eyes glittered more than the knife itself. "Live for you. Die for you. Burn down the world for you and take anything that stands in my way." He leaned down close to her ear and whispered, "I'll kill for you, *mia rosa,* and present their heart on a platter if it pleased you."

She moaned against him, his words engaging her soul. "And what would you do for me?" he asked.

She grabbed the knife from him, licking the blade. "Words aren't enough to show you, Darius. You'll find out soon enough."

He let out a throaty growl, almost snarling.

I can't wait to find out...

"But for now...we have business to take of."

Harmony

HARMONY LEFT HIS OFFICE with a plan in place. She felt like an entirely different person, the way she acted in there. And it felt *good*. She was finally letting her real self-shine thanks to Darius. He brought out something in her that had long been dormant and now she was blossoming. Padding back to her room, she grabbed her cell phone off the bed. It had been since before dinner yesterday that she had checked it, and of course she had a million missed calls and texts from Sofia.

I'm sorry, Harm...

I didn't mean to ruin our birthday. I just wanted to have a good time.

I don't understand why you're so upset. I didn't do anything wrong.

Please call me back?

Why aren't you answering me?

Will you call me? Alessandro wants to take us to dinner because he didn't get to celebrate our birthday.

Bingo. This was the "in" she needed, and she didn't even have to do any of the work.

She tapped her phone, and it began to ring.

"Harm...?"

"What do you want Sofia?" Her tone was laced with acid.

"Harm! Where have you been? I've been so worried about you!"

"Around. Running errands."

"For 2 days?"

"Well, if you actually stopped by my apartment instead of asking *mamma* and *papa,* you would know."

Harmony knew damn well her sister didn't bother to come check on her after their fight at the bar. She probably nursed a hangover all day and then decided to call her today to play nice and act like nothing happened.

"Harm, please. Alessandro wants to take us out for our birthday. A real nice place."

"And what *place* would that be?" Harmony scoffed. "We live in bumfuck Egypt in the middle of the mountains where Bigfoot and skinwalkers come out at night. Guys work for steel mill factories and the town looks like it's still in 1975. Where could he possibly take us that's *so* nice?"

"Altius in Pittsburgh."

Harmony almost dropped her phone. "Altius? The place with the $160 caviar?"

"Yeah! He said he'd treat the both of us."

And just where the hell did he get the money? As far as Harmony knew, her last tab on him said his own family wasn't paying his way after they found out what he did. No matter, what *did* matter was getting Darius near him to do the job. This was his ticket in.

"Alright. But I'll meet you there. It's almost an hour drive from here and I have to do a few things before I go."

"Okay. How about 8pm?"

"That's fine."

Harmony hung up the phone. This was going to be perfect.

Harmony

HARMONY WAS SILENT, the only sound was the roar of the restaurant and the clinking of her gold rings against her wine glass. She had picked out a slinky blue dress to match her eyes. She loved long dresses with the slit up the side, but this one barely covered her lower region. If she opened her legs everyone would get a show. A small slit went up both sides, stitched together with delicate black lace. The silken fabric rubbed against her large breasts with its custom built-in bra and chiffon straps.

She looked down at her phone. It was 8:10.

Why am I not surprised?

Taking another sip of liquid courage, she saw her phone light up. It was an unknown number texting her.

Late again?

She forgot she had given Darius her number before they left the mansion. She drove separately in her car so Alessandro wouldn't get suspicious. She knew Darius wasn't far behind and always had her in sight. She picked up her phone and started to type. *Yes. As always.*

She downed the rest of her glass and started to pour another from the bottle of Chateau Potelle. Eyeing up the menu, she was tempted to order the 2019 Spottswoode. Her phone lit up again.

Get the wine. If that bastard doesn't pay, I will.

Harmony smiled. *Oh really? Is that a date? How gentlemanly. You're mine,* mia rosa. *Anything for you.*

A chill went down her spine. Even reading those words was a sonata to her soul. *You're mine. I'm his.*

She called the waiter over to the table and asked for the bottle of Spottswoode. He seemed eager and pleased to bring her the selection.

A noise near the door pierced her ears. It was the familiar sound of her sister's laugh. *It's showtime.*

Sofia walked over to their table smiling and laughing. "Harmony!"

"You're late, Sofia."

"I'm sorry, we got held up."

Standing behind her was the vile in her throat: Alessandro. He looked as sleazy as ever with his greasy black hair and dark green eyes. His slim body made him look like a twig. She could tell the tailored suit he was wearing had seen some better days, nothing like when Sofia first sent her a pic of him. He looked nervous, sweat beading down his brow. He looked considerably paler than the last time she saw him.

"Anything wrong, Alessandro?" She cooed. "You don't look well."

"I'm fine." His voice was nails on a chalkboard. She couldn't stand it when he spoke, all she wanted to do was vomit.

She put on her fake smile and hid her disgust. "Sit down. I ordered wine, hope you don't mind. I was waiting for you to get here to order food."

Sofia plopped down on her chair. "Ugh! I'm starving. I hope they have some good steak. Oooo, maybe I'll get salmon!"

Sofia was lost in the menu, not paying any attention to her or Alessandro.

The rest of the night went without a hitch. Alessandro started to calm down and eased up after 4 glasses of wine. The three of them talked and laughed over steak tartare and their various meals of steak and salmon. They had just finished their fourth bottle of wine when coffee came around with a chocolate medley, crème brulee, and a strawberry pretzel for dessert. Sofia got Alessandro to reminisce about their time in Miami until she asked Harmony about her future plans.

"Summer's almost over and we're getting into fall Harm. What are you gonna do now that we're out of school?"

Harmony shrugged her shoulders. "I've been offered a position at my summer job so I think I might stick with that until I find something in the field."

Sofia giggled. "I don't know why you decided to go into criminal justice and cyber security, Harm. It's so...boring."

Harmony took a sip of her coffee. "I find it fascinating. Maybe I'll even go on to law school."

"Well...you go right ahead, Harm. Leaves for fun for the rest of us."

"I don't consider an undeclared major with a mass of stupid courses just so you could sleep around *fun*." Harmony muttered under her breath.

Sofia looked away from Alessandro to Harmony. "Did you say something, Harm?"

"Me?" Harmony put her hand on her chest and put her empty coffee cup back down on the saucer. "No, I didn't say anything."

Harmony placed her hand down next to her chair and moved her fingers to sign "L-E-A-V-E."

She knew Darius would see it wherever he was.

"Well, um...thank you for dinner Alessandro. That was sweet of you."

"Yeah...happy birthday." He slurred. *Perfect.*

The waiter came by with the check and placed it on the table. Alessandro looked at it and the sickening color came back into his cheeks. Harmony smiled. She bet that the bill was over two grand, since she purposely ordered the five-hundred-dollar wine bottles.

"I'll be right back, Sof. Gotta use the bathroom."

Alessandro practically ran from his chair to the back of the restaurant.

Harmony smiled. She knew Darius had to have seen him go toward the bathroom, and now it was just a waiting game for his signal.

Ten minutes had passed before Sofia started to worry.

"What's taking him so long?"

Almost immediately, her phone lit up. Sofia looked down and saw it was a text from Alessandro.

"Huh. He said something's come up and for us to go on ahead."

"Oh." Harmony feigned. "Hope it's nothing serious."

"I don't think it is. Harm, can you take me home?"

"Absolutely, sis."

Harmony and Sofia got up and left the restaurant, walking out to her car. The entire ride home Sofia was chattering incessantly. Harmony wished the wine would kick in a little more and she would shut the fuck up. An hour later, she pulled up to Sofia's door.

Sofia smiled and reached over to the driver's side, hugging Harmony.

"And what's that for?" Harmony quipped.

"For being a great sister."

You have no idea...

Harmony turned back toward the road, trying to hide the softness in her face. "Thanks."

Sofia got out of the car and looked back at Harmony. "Do you think he's ok? He does this sometimes, but he's never left me to catch a ride home."

"I'm sure he's fine. Probably an important work thing or something."

"Ok. See you soon?" There was hope in her voice.

"Yeah." Harmony said dryly. With that, she pulled off and made her way to start the half-hour drive back toward Darius' mansion. If he was just here for a hit, she was curious how the hell he had a mansion in the middle of nowhere near the mountains. She'd have to ask about it later.

Rounding the corner up the long and winding macadam road, the mansion loomed in the distance. She pulled up to the gate, showing her badge to Tony the security guard to let her in.

"He's already made his way to the cottage, Miss Catrone."

Efficient much? Then again, she had purposely driven a bit slower on the way home and she had to go out of her way to drop Sofia off at her apartment. She drove up the road to the 7-car attached garage and pulled into the one open door. The whirring of the garage door was white-noise as she got out and made her way to the back of the house. Going through the large living room area from the foyer to the dining room, there was a massive sunporch leading out to an even larger patio. The patio was complete with lounge chairs, plush cushions, an inground fire pit, built-in bar and grilling area, and a cabana. Her heels clacked against the brick and cement. A small stone path from the patio led to a shed the size of a small outhouse a few feet away. She squeaked open the wooden door and stepped inside. Locking the door behind her, a caged wall came down the floor began to move. Down, deep down she went, the elevator taking her a few feet underground. When it stopped, the cage lifted open revealing a clean, well-lit tunnel encased in cement. A few feet from her was a railing and a moving travelator. She stepped onto the belt and leaned against the railing, the travelator taking her down the tunnel faster than her feet could move. It wasn't long until she reached the end. A bank of large, sealed-off steel doors lined the walls. She walked to the right towards the closest door and knocked twice. She heard the wizzes and clanks of the automatic lock coming undone. Looking up, a camera was right above her. She waved, then the door swung open. Stepping inside, she couldn't help but smile. Darius stood behind Alessandro tied tightly to a Saint Andrews cross. He was putting on his leather gloves when she walked in. Alessandro's head was down, blood dripping from his mouth. He was stripped down to his boxers, and she could see bruises were already appearing on his ribs.

Harmony walked up to Darius and rubbed her hands over his chest. "Who said you could start the fun without me?"

"I'm sorry, *mia rosa*, I got a little excited." He purred. Darius grabbed her around her waist and nibbled on her neck, his tongue soothing where his teeth had just been.

His name escaped her lips with a moan of pleasure. "Darius."

She didn't know why his touch and teases were turning her on so much, especially in front of Alessandro's broken and bleeding body. But it was hot, and she loved every minute of it.

"I'll take care of that pussy later, *mia rosa;* right now we have work to do."

"What if we do both at the same time?"

She had no idea why she said that. The thought ripped through her mouth before she could stop herself from vocalizing it. She looked back at him, ready to apologize, but all she saw was a hunger. She couldn't tell if it was for her, for the thrill and power of having Alessandro in his grasp, or both. Either way, she felt something deep down inside her rise and whisper to her, *take both*.

Suddenly, her mouth was on his, her tongue exploring his mouth. He moaned against her, she felt his cock grow hard, the touch searing her bare skin. She knew he was battling with himself to stay on task but fuck her senseless. She broke away from him, and the look on his face told her the decision he had made.

Darius

WHAT THE HELL WAS THIS woman doing? He went through careful planning and dealing with his men to grab Alessandro and bring him back to his bunker to have this moment. A job was to be done. But here she was, walking in and asking, no, demanding with her body and her mouth for him to fuck her and kill Alessandro at the same time. His body shuddered, his cock standing up at attention and so hard it hurt. The pain and pleasure of his large third fucking leg was pressing against his pants was almost unbearable. He wanted to spring it from its confines and show it to her, let her play. If this is what love is really like, he'd take it. Harmony was weaving her way into his heart forever. If she wanted to play while working, so be it. After all, all work and no play made Darius a dull boy. He grabbed the back of her head, freeing her hair from the confines of her pins and hair ties that held up her curls. Her long locks cascaded down her back and she shook her head, the bouncing curls spraying over her shoulders. He kissed her back, grabbing her ass and slightly pulling her dress up over her hips.

"Let's play, my little spitfire."

Her eyes fluttered as she whispered, "Yes, sir, let's play."

Walking back over to Alessandro, he smacked his cheek with the back of his hand. His one eye was already starting to swell shut from a punch to the face.

"Wake the fuck up." He growled. "You're going to watch this before I get rid of you, you rapist bastard."

He didn't exactly know his thought process with that statement. Maybe Alessandro was so fucked up and battered he'd think he was fucking Sofia instead of Harmony. Not the smartest idea he's ever had, but with Harmony around stirring every emotion and nerve in his body, nothing made sense anymore.

A small chair was off to the corner. Harmony had already grabbed it and dragged it over to be close enough she could touch him while he worked. Normally he'd quickly take out his victims and dispose of their bodies before anyone knew they were missing. This man...no...this man was in for a treat. He hurt the woman he loved, her sister, and her best friend. He was going to suffer as they had suffered.

He felt like a brick went into his chest with the realization. He *loved* her. He'd do anything to make her happy, to please her, burn his way through anything while walking through the fire to get to her. He didn't care how much blood he had to spill as long as she was safe and happy....with him.

He looked back before he began, watching her. The heat was evident in her eyes. She was a strong woman who could manipulate people, hide her emotions, and make deals with the best of the *capos*, but she couldn't hide her emotions from him. She loved him back.

Harmony

SHE KNEW HE SAW IT, the love in her eyes. It was fast, it was sudden, but she knew she couldn't live without him. He was the Hades to her Persephone, her Joker to his Harley, her Mickey to her Mallory Knox. They were fucked up, but the insanity of their lives fit together perfectly. Two people involved with the blood and underground of America, the politics of the Mafia. It was business. Together, they could bridge the gaps between the four families in Los Angeles, Miami, New York, and Chicago. They could build an empire of peace between them. The thought of business was taking over until she saw Darius pull out his bag of toys. He walked over to a small radio built into the wall. He flipped the switch and it began to play Tchaikovsky's Symphony No. 5 in E minor, Op. 64. She licked her lips as he sliced through

Alessandro's skin, small knicks that just barely bled. Alessandro watched them, spewing out curses in Italian. The curses turned to screams when Darius placed salt on the wounds. The screams ran down her spine, filling her with the justice her family deserved. She got up from the chair and gently placed her hand on Darius' back.

"*Mia rosa*, I'm trying to work." He cooed softly.

Harmony smiled. "Please, *mi amore*, let me play too."

He smiled back at her and bowed, his hand gesturing to the bag. She reached down and pulled out a small bat just big enough for her. It was light, but mighty. Casually she walked up to Alessandro and swung, the bat crashing into his ribs. He strained against the ropes, trying to hold his chest from the agonizing pain.

"This is for Paola." She took her stiletto heel and jabbed it into his cock. As she twisted it, he let out a curdling scream of agonizing pain.

"You will never harm my family again. Don Tagliatti sends his regards."

Harmony walked away from him and motioned to Darius to let him take care of the rest, but not before she gently wrapped her hand around his and brought the knife up to her lips. He quickly froze, not letting the bloody knife get any closer to her.

"No, *mia rosa,* you don't want this filth near your perfect lips. I have something more worthy of that for you later."

Sitting down on the chair, she watched him work. She felt the heat grow between her thighs, her pussy dripping wet. He was so hot and sexy when he worked. The determination in his black eyes, his skill and precision, it made her want to get on her knees and suck his cock while he cut into Alessandro. The only thing that stopped her was she didn't want Alessandro's blood dripping on her and possibly getting in her mouth.

Darius was in the process of ripping off Alessandro's fingernails when she opened her legs and pulled her panties off. The Allegro con anima was coming to an end as the Andante cantabile con alcuna licenza began. Her fingers stroked her clit, sending her eyes almost rolling in the back of her head. Slowly she pushed one, then two fingers in and began pumping inside herself. She let out a loud moan which caught Darius and Alessandro's attention.

"Love, right now?"

"I'm sorry...it's just...when you work it's so hot, baby."

Alessandro was panting, moaning from the pain that was being inflicted on him. Darius looked back at Alessandro then back to Harmony. *Guess it's later.*

"Don't die on me."

Darius walked over to Harmony, grabbing her and pulling her to her knees. He unbuckled his belt, his pants falling to the floor. His cock bounced in front of her, thick, hard, and ready for the taking. She quickly took it into her mouth, sheathing it to the hilt. He let out a moan as his hand pushed against the back of her head. His cock was so deep in her mouth she was able to slip out her tongue from between it and her teeth to lick at his balls against her chin.

"Good girl." He groaned. That only turned her on even more.

"Now, please yourself while I fill that filthy mouth of yours." She spread her legs wide, using one hand to push inside her wet and dripping pussy while the other wound around his back to steady herself as she bobbed back and forth, her mouth being filled and unfilled. He helped guide her, thrusting himself in and out of her mouth.

She could feel him tensing, almost on the verge of coming. "That's enough."

He quickly pulled out then turned her, putting her on all fours, bending her over the chair.

Darius turned back to Alessandro. "Watch."

Alessandro had no choice. He wasn't able to shut his eyes. Harmony didn't know why, but she was too busy wanting to orgasm from Darius' cock to ask.

Darius leaned down next to Harmony's ear, pushing up her dress around her waist. He expertly slipped one hand into the top of her dress and pulled out one breast, then the other. He squeezed them and played with the nipples until they peaked. She moaned and tried to rub her ass against his cock, needing the friction to relieve her aching lower lips. He pressed it against her opening.

"Do you want this?"

"Yes, please, yes," she whispered, her throat dry.

"I can't hear you, *mia rosa*. Do you want this cock deep in your little cunt?"

"Yes! Please, daddy, yes, I need you." She screamed.

"Your wish is my command, your majesty."

He slammed himself into her, the pleasure and pressure so intense she thought she'd orgasm and pass out at the same time. He pumped hard inside her, the friction causing her to scream. She was never one to be very vocal, just some moaning, but *Dio,* this man had her crying and screaming his name. She couldn't take it anymore. She was on the verge, almost at the edge. She didn't want to come unless he did. He must have understood her because he pumped harder inside her, then slow, deep penetration as they moaned together, calling each other's name. The finale—Andante maestoso - Allegro vivace—started. She climaxed over his cock while he filled her up with his seed, all while the climax of the orchestral piece occurred. He pulled out of her, dripping with their juices, while the cream ran down her legs. He walked over to a small door like the ones in the doctor's office when they ask for a piss sample. In the door were two wet cloths. Darius cleaned himself up, then walked over to her, rubbing down her thighs and ass. The cool, wet cloth felt good on her skin. She pulled down her dress and he pulled up his pants, putting himself back together. Darius gently kissed her on the lips.

"Do you feel better?"

Harmony smiled through her satisfied haze. "Yes, *mi amore.*"

"Good. Now let your *amore* work."

Harmony sat on the chair, happy and content as she watched Darius walk back over to Alessandro. He had watched the entire thing, his eyes a mix of pain, shock, and fear.

"Wha...what...about...Sofia...why?"

She cocked her head. "Sofia? How cute, *mi amore.* He's so out of his fucking mind he thinks I'm my sister. Wrong sister asshole, it's Harmony. Oh, I'm sure I can come up with an easy enough explanation for her. After all, you just *love* to use women until you're done with them, right, Alessandro?"

He never got another word out. Darius' hand was around his neck, crushing his vocal chords and cutting off his air supply. Five minutes later, after slowly squeezing and adding a small amount of pressure each minute, the light finally died from Alessandro's eyes.

Harmony smiled wickedly. Justice had been served. She got up and walked over to Darius, slowly kissing him on the neck.

"Want me to help get rid of him?"

Darius turned back and smiled. "No. Eddie needs to redeem himself, and Marco and Vincenzo can handle it."

He bent down and kissed her, long and hard.

"You understand you're mine forever? I'd have to kill you if you leave."

She looked back up at him and lifted her hand, running her fingers through his hair. The small light in the room caught it just right, making it look like a raging fire.

"I love you too much to leave you. Besides, you're mine forever too. You see what happens when you hurt *Papà* Tagliatti's family."

Darius reached down to cup her breast and gently grab the back of her neck. "Get upstairs," he groaned. "We're not done yet."

Harmony didn't say a word after he released his grip. She took one glance back at Alessandro, the blood dripping from his lifeless body. Darius smiled at her.

"Not today *mia rosa*. No blood play. I don't know what kind of filthy disease this fucker has and I'm not risking it with you."

How did he know what she was thinking? Using some of the blood as lube would've been *hot,* but he was right. She picked up her panties and sashayed to the door, leaving him to speak with Eddie, Marco, and Vincenzo who were standing outside the door.

"He's all yours, boys."

Alessandro that is...because Darius is all mine.

After getting back up to the house, she grabbed her phone from her purse on the foyer table. She walked over to the living room and sat down on the same couch Darius had just fucked her on the day before. Pressing two buttons, the phone rang.

A man answered, his voice ragged and withered with age. *"Harmony!* Mia figlia, *I trust it's done."*

"Si, Papà. It's done."

"That's good. When will you be back to visit us? Paola misses you and I need my best capo *by my side."*

"Soon, *Papà.* There's been a change of plans."

"Oh? Dimmi.*"*

"It's a long story, but I fell in love."

"Bring him to Chicago. I want to meet him."

"The thing is you already know him."

She could almost feel the old man smiling behind the phone.

"I never expected you and Darius together. He's a good man in our line of work."

"Papà, I have a proposition. Can we meet with you soon? I think I have an idea to bring peace to the four families."

"Be here in two days. Love you, figlia.*"*

"Love you too."

She hung up the phone and felt someone watching her. She turned around and saw Darius leaning against the doorjamb to the sun porch.

He looked amazing in his all-black suit, the only contrast being his purple tie and small green sixteenth note cufflinks. The man certainly loved his blacks, purples, and greens. His wide-brimmed black fedora was cocked to one side a bit, a small white feather was stuck within the ribbon.

"Hides the blood better."

It was almost as if he could read her thoughts.

Harmony scoffed. "I'm sure you have a great dry cleaner to take care of that."

"I do. But right now, I need to take care of you."

She smiled, licking her lips. She was his, and he was hers. She couldn't wait to start their empire, together.

Don't miss out!

Visit the website below and you can sign up to receive emails whenever Ashley Bríon publishes a new book. There's no charge and no obligation.

https://books2read.com/r/B-A-CVQP-QYHWC

BOOKS 2 READ

Connecting independent readers to independent writers.

Did you love *Music of Seduction*? Then you should read *Illusion at Midnight*[1] by Ashley Bríon!

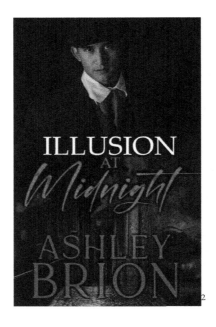

[2]

After spending centuries searching for his lost love, Andre finds her on her last reincarnation as Lily Cordova.

Lily, a witch, has long awaited his arrival but is unprepared for the decision he brings her. As a vampire, he cannot die and follow her into the afterlife once this lifecycle takes her from him. Andre must woo Lily and reignite the memories from her past lives in hopes she will finally choose him.

---

1. https://books2read.com/u/mKdXnd

2. https://books2read.com/u/mKdXnd

As the hurricane barrels their way, Lily has a choice to make: let it sweep her away, leaving her in the afterlife forever, or let Andre turn her into a vampire.

"Though short, this novel is an emotional rollercoaster that will leave readers satisfied and hopeful. Ashley Brion's writing is truly unparalleled." -Robin Ginther-Venneri, owner of Robin's Reviews and KIPS Publishing

Read more at:

https://www.slucas0.wixsite.com/authorashleybrion.

About the Author

Ashley Brion is a 2013, 2015, and 2019 BA, MA, and MFA graduate in English and Creative Writing. Ashley has a long history of French and English heritage. She is bilingual speaking both French and English. She spends her free time gaming with her friends, acting, tap dancing, practicing yoga, and playing with her pets. Ashley embraces her love of history and different cultures through her writings, is autistic, and is a "social justice warrior" advocating for LGBTQIA+ and BIPOC rights. Her favorite holidays are Halloween and Christmas and enjoys a cup of sake every evening.

Follow her on all her socials and sign up for her monthly newsletter on her website.

TikTok: @Jokergurl09

Facebook:

www.facebook.com/authorashleybrion

Instagram:

www.instagram.com/@authorashleybrion

Bookbub:

https://www.bookbub.com/authors/ashley-brion
Read more at:
    https://www.slucas0.wixsite.com/authorashleybrion.

Printed in Great Britain
by Amazon